# The Lighthouse

Jeremy Schliewe

**The Lighthouse**
by Jeremy Schliewe

ISBN: 978-1-908125-79-8

Cover Art by David Rix

Publication Date: October 2019

# The Lighthouse

I tend to think of all stories, at least the ones that appeal to me, as having some tragic element of separation.  Each story of this type, though the details may vary, evokes a central image in my mind — that of a person suspended in darkness, mouth shaping a silent scream (for these images are unaccompanied by sound), arms outstretched as if grasping for a buoy in the nothingness, as they are inexorably pulled away into the vacuum of the distance.  An image sometimes invades my consciousness: that of the above scenario only with the generic representation of personhood replaced by the very real features of somebody who has been very much a concrete player in my own life.  It is the beginning of a process that, though again the details may vary, will pull this very real person (a friend, a partner, a family member) out of my life, more often in slow increments than by a sudden yank. There is some underlying universal force at work that drives people apart thus and I feel that, in a sense, it is this force that is the source of all the loneliness and misery in the world. I said that this phenomenon appealed to some dark sensibility I carry, that it was a *type* of story, but I have long held the suspicion that every story, if one were to look closely enough, contains this terrible element.

It was the middle of the night when I got the call from my brother, saying he had been arrested for trying to break into the lighthouse that stood sentry where the edge of our hometown met the waters of Lake Michigan. He sounded tired; there was a gruffness in his voice that I had not anticipated, as he was ten years my junior. It had been a handful of years since I had last seen him. I hated to think of him as having aged, if for no better reason than it meant that I had aged as well and I, if the sequence of events played out as they so often did, was first in the queue for death. But he was my little brother, taller than me and, if his habits of the past years had not changed, heavily bearded.

I loved Charles and I felt that for the bulk of our lives we were greatly similar. The years, however, had put a space between our core temperaments. At a glance, one would probably not assume Charles and I were brothers (we were in fact half-brothers as we did not share the same father). Despite our difference in age, we enjoyed a close friendship that began when Charles became a young man (and insisted that we stopped calling him "Charlie" or, perhaps even more irritating to him, "Cubby.")

"They want to press charges," came his voice over the phone, pulling me out my reminiscence. "Can you come help?"

I assumed that, strapped for cash as he perpetually was, he needed money for bail. Though often destitute, Charles rarely hit me up. Perhaps he was too proud, perhaps he feared a lecture from me – I had gone through a phase some years ago, around the time our mother died, when I decided that I must take a more parental role in regard to him. I would hover over him each night, trying to make sure he did his homework (in which he showed next to no interest) and make suggestions to him for possible career paths ("You're pretty good with computers. Do you think you might want to go to school for that someday?") These attempts were often rather strained – I was not equipped for the role of guardian and Charles, perhaps still reeling over the loss of our mother, hated school with fervor. I would occasionally, out of sheer frustration, drag him bodily to the dining room table, upon which I had arranged his schoolbooks, and sit him down, hovering over him in grim silence as he, with much difficulty, trudged through the battery of homework. I would chime in when I could, but his lessons were the stuff of ancient history to me, requiring an aptitude for rote memorization and mathematical concepts that would not prove useful later in life. I would often find myself as frustrated as my little brother, perhaps even more so because I had not asked to be thrust into such a role.

Our mother, twice divorced, was beginning to sink into the illness that, unbeknownst to us, would take her life. Charles's father lived across town in a two-story house that had a dark gray countenance and seemed much too large for a man whose primary function was to drink himself into a comfortable oblivion.

But if it were money Charles was after, why would he request that I go to him? I had some vacation banked at work. I called the answering service and informed my employer that an emergency had come up and I would be gone for a short but unforeseeable amount of time, promising to call with an update as soon as I had a better idea of what exactly was going on.

I packed a small suitcase and booked a flight. Fortunately, as sunrise was only a few hours away, I was able to take an Uber to the airport immediately. There was no airport in the town in which I grew up. The nearest was an almost abandoned affair that offered only a handful of flights on any given day. Since I had no family other than my brother left and few, if any, friends remaining in my hometown, I grabbed a rental car at the airport and made the twenty-minute drive there and parked in front of the police station where I filled out some paperwork and posted the four-hundred dollar bond.

It was no colossal sum, but I was certain it was more than my brother, who spent most of his days in unemployment, could afford.

Charles, escorted by a police officer, emerged from a door next to the front counter. His sandy blonde hair was disheveled, his beard untrimmed, and his t-shirt wrinkled as if he had slept in it. His appearance, however, caused me no alarm. I was used to seeing him with all his frayed edges on display. He did not look any older than his thirty years. In fact, he looked positively boyish to me. Members of our family – the ones who kept their drinking in moderation anyway – had a tendency to not show their age. Charles looked like a lanky boy in a russet beard. He peered down through his black-framed eyeglasses at me and offered an apologetic grin. He outstretched his arms and gave me a hug, patting me on the back in an exaggerated manner, as if he were mocking the type of nervous embrace people sometimes engaged in, as if we were young again and goofing around in our comfortable old way.

"Thanks for coming," he said.

What choice did I have? Aside from an uncle on his father's side, for whom he occasionally did odd jobs, I was the only family he had left.

"You might not want to stay with me," he said. "Sorry, but the place is a bit of a mess."

The place he referred to was his father's, which he had inherited after his dad failed to negotiate a turn after a night of drinking and drove his car into a lake. The timing was unfortunate – as if this sort of thing ever happens at a good time – as Charles, well into his floundering twenties, was rather close to being thrown out on the street by his dad for his now well-established lack of ambition. The house was the ultimate break. With the last vestige of authority gone from his life and the keys to his own private castle now firmly in hand, he was free to continue unencumbered down his non-path, with only property tax, home repairs (which I was certain he did not keep up), and nourishment to concern himself with. Apart from the house, he had received a modest inheritance from his father, who in life was a schoolteacher; anything he had received from our mother I was certain he had already gone through.

Charles did not have a car. With the exception of the bitter winter months, which were long and made bone-bitingly cold by our proximity to Lake Michigan, our small town was easily traversable by foot.

I dropped Charles off at his father's house – no, *his* house – before heading back to the highway that bisected our town, to check into a hotel. We made small talk as I drove, dancing around the subject of his arrest. Perhaps he was not yet ready to open up about it. Struggling with the intense wave of nostalgia and sorrow that came with return visits to my hometown, I did not feel the urge to plunge headlong into deep waters just yet. It was late afternoon when I dropped him off. The plan was for me to get a room, take a short nap, and pick my brother up at six o'clock so we could grab something to eat.

Having said our temporary goodbyes, I looked over at the passenger seat and noticed that it was covered with a fine dusting of sand, a remnant of my brother's recent adventure with the lighthouse.

I checked into the Days Inn. The inviting jewel with the glassed-in indoor pool that it had been in my youth had lost much of its luster. My room seemed dingy, run down and water-stained. It mattered not. It was a temporary measure and its flaws evaporated as I fell into a heavy sleep.

When I awoke I was seized by the momentary panic of not knowing where I was. The heavy curtains had obliterated all traces of light from the room. The events of the past eighteen hours came back to me. My mouth was dry and I felt the oppressive weight of a depression that had settled upon me. Groggily, I fought my way out of bed and went to the window and pushed the curtain aside. It was dark out, I had overslept. Looking out, the traffic was light on the highway. September was approaching and the tourist season was winding down. I called my brother – I could not text him as he had no mobile phone – and let him know I was on my way.

We got a table at a pizzeria that had been a longtime favorite of ours. I ordered a couple of beers from the server but Charles requested a Coke instead.

"I don't drink anymore," he told me after the server had left. "For reasons I'm sure you understand." Then, changing the subject. "Do you know they want to take down the catwalk?"

He was referring to a structure on the pier, a centipedal wrought-iron affair that ran its length, from the beginning of the pier to the red sentry of the lighthouse at the end. At night, capped with cylindrical lights, it was indeed a beautiful sight, an icon of my boyhood, a symbol of our community. When I was a boy (and Charles little more than a baby), there had been a movement to raise funds to "Help Save the Catwalk" – the slogan adorned t-shirts and bumper stickers for a couple of summers. The effort was successful. The funds were acquired and the catwalk remained for a couple more decades.

The news hadn't reached me, of course. I was not in the habit of checking in with the hometown paper's website. Any news it offered seemed somehow quaint and insular – perhaps I felt above it all, now that I had moved away and made my place in a proper city, and that restoration efforts in my hometown were a trifling thing and mattered not to someone who had a larger sense of the world, to someone who no longer questioned the idea of progress.

The pizza arrived. I ordered a second beer. Charles and I spent some time reminiscing – though our childhood was not particularly idyllic, we were, with the passing of years, able to see many of its events through a humorous, if dark, lens.

With a second beer in me, I felt ready to address the potentially uncomfortable subject that had thus far gone unacknowledged.

"The lighthouse," I said. "What happened?"

Charles shifted in his seat.

"I don't know," he said. "I was out one night. I wasn't drinking or anything. Just restless, I guess, so I went for a walk. I made the turn at Harbor Avenue and there it was, at the end of the pier, the catwalk all strung with lights. It was unusually warm and it was just kind of a natural destination, the farthest west you could go without getting wet."

He wiped his mouth with a napkin and pushed his plate away. "I got to thinking about it," he continued. "All our lives, it's just been standing there. You never see anyone go in or come out of it. What's inside of it? A spiral staircase going up to the top? I suppose you could live in it, or someone like me could, someone with no wife or family. It would be no worse than a small apartment. I guess I just wanted to have a look inside, to see if I could move in.  Or to see if someone already had.  Maybe one of those people who drowned off the pier.  Maybe all of them.

"They call it a beacon," he said. "Something to guide you.  That wasn't lost on me either.  How many ships are there these days that actually need that thing?  It's like it was becoming useless as far as its original intent went and found another way to fulfill its purpose.  To tell you the truth, I can't stop thinking about it."


It was late, but I was in a state of exhaustion from the plane ride and my too-long nap.  I did not want my brother to think I was bored of his company, but I felt an overpowering urge to return to my room and surrender to the special brand of oblivion that only a hotel room can offer.

However, he soon saved me the potential awkwardness of admitting to my tiredness.

"I don't mean to be rude," he said, "but would it be all right if you just brought me home? I think I need to lie down for a while."

I had long worn a sort of façade around my brother under the assumption that he looked to me as a role model.  I tried to represent myself as the very picture of health, energy, and enthusiasm in the hope that he would internalize and make real in himself what was counterfeit in me.  I was able to justify this deception because I told myself

I truly wanted what was best for him, and did not want my darker traits to find purchase in his mind, which was back then largely that of a child. My role-modeling, however, was unsuccessful. In his teenage years, a personality emerged that one would never mistake for that of innocence. As a teenager, Charles became rebellious. There were frequent clashes with our mother, failing grades, and a complete disregard for curfews and other half-hearted attempts at structure imposed by our frustrated mother. My attempts to steer him back to the straight and narrow were redoubled until, out of sheer frustration (and, undoubtedly, a lack of experience) I gave up completely. It was, after all, time for my reluctant move to college – the pressure to do so was due in large part to my own father to whom Charles, perhaps to his disadvantage, had no blood ties.

I dropped Charles off at his inherited home. He did not invite me in, even for a customary tour. It was this house that made Charles my half-brother rather than my brother, for I did not know what went on inside its walls. I then made the short drive back to the hotel. Once I settled in, I was gripped by an incredible restlessness. I put on a robe, padded down the hallway to the poolroom, hoping to get a quick soak in the hot tub, but found that the area was locked at nine o'clock.

I went back to my room, sat on the bed, and idly flipped through the television channels but was unable to settle on anything. I put on a t-shirt, jeans and a light jacket. A drive by the lake would perhaps kill some time until the ability to sleep returned.

I approached from the south side of town, taking the long meandering road past the wooded park and cemetery, which had always given me an uneasy feeling at night. The road made a final descending curve before it straightened and jogged along a sandy stretch of Lake Michigan shoreline. The beach was dark, gray sand broken here and there by a patch of reedy beach grass, the lake beyond black with soft mantles of gray foam. It was a wavy night on the usually calm lake. On the right, the dunes climbed and trees grew, the greenery of foliage dissected by long wooden staircases, the homes of the town's wealthy inserted like cartridges into the hill.

Down the road, the State Park began. Here appeared the first signs of life in the otherwise sleepy town. Despite the lateness of the season, there were still quite a few RVs parked at the campsites at the edge of the beach, little rectangles with yellow lights glowing inside, pop-up awnings strung with Christmas lights, or the undulating glow of campfires reflecting off the aluminum housing of the campers, families huddled around with hotdogs and marshmallows and cans of beer for the grown ups.

A DNR pickup truck made a lonely circuit around the park and the adjacent lot, which began where the beach met the pier and stretched east with the channel. There were almost no cars at all in the far lot, which at the height of summer was often completely filled.

As the park boundary ended, the lakefront again became dark, except for the cylindrical lights that seemed to float above the pier in metered intervals to the lighthouse, its roguish eye sweeping the night sky with its beam.

What was the source of my brother's fascination? Surely, as far as lighthouses went, it was a fine structure and one intertwined inextricably with the mythology of my youth, but wasn't it just that – a structure that, through the mind's innate tendency to make associations between memories and objects (I suppose this is the root of nostalgia), had been imbued with a greater significance than was merited?

I was nearing the end of my town's allotment of beachfront and was about to follow the natural bend in the road that would point me back toward my hotel when, under the clean white lights of the catwalk, I saw a lone figure walking the pier. The person was lanky and, as if to apologize for his extra portion of height, walked with his shoulders stooped and head held low. There was a shuffle in the gait that, despite my distance from the pier, was unmistakable. It could be none other than my brother Charles.

I turned the car around and, since the entrance to the State Park was closed due to the late hour, left my car at the gate, hoping that the DNR agent would not see me parked illegally as he made his rounds.

Skirting the gate, I climbed the small dune that served as a natural boundary to the parking lot. I ran for the pier, the only sound beyond the quiet crashing of waves was the soles of my shoes scuffing across the ground. I was out of breath by the time I had reached the corner of the lot, where one edge met the sand of the beach and the other the beginning of the pier.

My brother receded into the distance. His pace was unhurried, but he had made great progress toward the lighthouse in the time it had taken me to park.

"Charles!" I called out as I began my run down the length of the pier, but my voice was swallowed up in the great emptiness above the lake, lost in the rhythmic sloshing of the waves. He walked, slouching forward, hands thrust into the pockets of his beige thrift store Harrington jacket.

A gray-blue watercolor wash was all I could see in the semi-dark. I called out again, before deciding that my efforts were better put into running. I did not go full speed for fear I would slip on an unseen wet patch and tumble headlong into the lake. The waves got choppy with the approaching autumn; one heard stories of drownings every year.

It did not take long to catch up to him, given his moderate pace. I said his name again and put a hand on his shoulder. I assumed I would startle him, a voice, the sensation of a touch in the darkness, but he hardly reacted at all, turning to me as if I had awoken him from a dream.

"What are you doing here?" I asked.

He blinked slowly, as if to bat away sleep from his eyes. "I'm on a walk."

"You know you're not supposed to be out here. It doesn't look good." I began to feel like I was lecturing him, so I stopped.

"Come on," I said. "I'll give you a ride home."

Minding the headlights of the DNR truck (the last thing my brother needed was another ticket for trespassing), we made our way back to the rental car.

"Do you want to go get a coffee somewhere?" my brother asked.

"It's nearly midnight," I said, momentarily forgetting that he was now a teetotaler.

"I just don't want to go home."

There was a café that kept late hours on the main tourist stretch. We ordered drinks, mine decaf, and took a seat in the corner. We were nearly the only customers.

Why did he not want to go home? Maybe he was getting lonely as his youth wound down. I tried to imagine his home life – a television, an outdated computer, stacks of books (Henry Miller,

Alan Watts, DT Suzuki – some he had picked up from my younger reading habits, some he had discovered on his own). A life of reading, movies, video games, the internet. A life of the mind, but with plentiful convenient distractions for when the mind became burdensome. Maybe there were women, maybe internet friends – the world wasn't going anywhere, it always waited outside the door – one could rejoin the human race at one's convenience, if willing to shoulder the quotidian annoyances of a regular existence. Why not hole up? Why not turn your back on everything? In solitude, one can see the world however one wants to see it. Outside forces, forever bent on proselytizing their version of reality, seldom arrive with happy news.

"Sometimes the place just feels too big for me," my brother said, as if he were reading my thoughts. "Sometimes I just want the walls to be closer, more intimate." He blew on his coffee, a cup of black drip. "Sometimes I just have to get out."

"You were heading to the lighthouse."

He shrugged.

"You should know better," I said. "With a court date coming up and all."

"I was just walking."

"Well, this town may be small, but there are plenty of other places you could go," I said, with perhaps a bit too much of the lecturer in my tone. A silence hung between us. I felt like my own father, as if I had suddenly inherited his style of dealing with undesirable behavior, complete with readymade lines of dialogue.

"Look, I'm sorry," I said. "I don't know what to do. Or say. I'm not good at this. I know we don't get to see each other as much as we would like. Things aren't like what they were when we were younger and that's good in a lot of ways, but it's also not good. I feel we've suffered as a family, as brothers, but also as friends. What I mean to say is that I'm here. I'm here now and if there's anything I can do, anything you need to tell me or talk about, I am here. I am here and I am listening."

"Did you know that the lighthouse was built in the summer of 1838, on the recommendation of G.J. Prendergast?" He produced a pouch of tobacco from his jacket pocket and began with fastidious precision to roll a cigarette. "Rogers and Burnett came from Milwaukee to build the structure, under the supervision of the reverend William Montague Ferry. For the pier, they imported stone quarried in Green Bay, Wisconsin, which was renowned for its quality."

He scooted back in his chair and stood up, indicating the cigarette he held between his fingers.

"Excuse me," he said. He walked outside and, shielding his lighter flame from the wind with a cupped hand, lighted his cigarette.

What was with this rote recitation of facts? It was the type of information that aging local historians prided themselves in knowing, not 30-year-old bearded hipsters. What was his fascination? I surveyed the table. He had downed his coffee while mine was still half finished. Outside the glass storefront, I saw my brother exhale a plume of white smoke, his gaze fixed westward where the lighthouse was still visible in the distance.

My time in Michigan was winding down. I had fulfilled my duty as older brother and could go back home secure in the knowledge that I had done the right thing. There was still the trial, of course, but I could be of little help in that regard. I booked a return flight for early the next morning. Now that the weekend was upon us I could forget, for a brief moment anyway, the responsibilities of my job and enjoy my hometown. It would leave me a full day to revisit some of my old haunts and spend some time with my brother.

There were a handful of sites I wanted to hit. It was a sunny, crisp Saturday that would possibly warm up into one of the last pleasant weekends of the season. In my haste, I had forgotten to pack my running shoes, but our town was easily traversable on foot. It was seven in the morning; my brother, if his old habits held sway, was almost certainly still asleep. This afforded me some time to tick one piece of nostalgic business off my list – a walk through Duncan's Woods, a small parcel of forested park that sat in the middle of town.

It wasn't much more than a couple of trails wending through a wooded, hilly patch of land, but if one went far enough in (and if the motor noise of passing cars was widely enough spaced), one could feel that they had severed ties with the civilized world. I encountered, as one almost certainly does when following the southernmost trail, the large chain link fence that separates the woods from the town cemetery. I rested for a moment leaning into that fence and looking through it at the manicured lawns, the neat rolling hills, and the gray marble teeth of the gravestones.

I looked at my phone. Only an hour had passed since I had left the hotel. I could swing by my brother's house, wake him, and walk with him to the Harbor House, a local breakfast spot I had been meaning to revisit.

It was less than a mile to my brother's so I made the distance in a short time. The sleepy town was starting to come alive. Cars loaded with out-of-towners took short cuts through neighborhoods to stake an early claim at the beach, gambling on a warm afternoon. Before long, I found myself knocking on my brother's front door. As expected, there was no response. I walked around to the side of the two-story structure and looked up at the half-open window that had belonged to his bedroom when he was a teenager and, due to frequent clashes with our mother, opted to move in with his father. I called out his name, not entirely sure if he still slept there. There was no response. I walked back to the front door. The lawn was dry and ragged, in need of water and a mowing. The white paint that trimmed the windows was starting to peel. If my brother's neglect of home maintenance continued, it would be in just a few years a shabby sight indeed.

I rapped at the door again with no better results. Knowing he usually left the front porch unlocked, I opened it in order to try knocking on the proper door to the house, which, if still asleep, he would be more likely to hear.

I stepped into the narrow porch, which allotted just enough space for a beat-up old couch and end table. On the end table was an ashtray filled with the butts of hand-rolled cigarettes and a stack of books (Miller, Watts, the Tao Te Ching, Nietzsche, *Man and His Symbols*, something about chaos magick, and a few books on local history I did not recognize). I knocked on the inner door and called out again. There was something on the other side of the door that I could not comprehend, a deadness that ate up my knocking, that would not allow the sound to travel throughout the house to reach him, if indeed he were even home.

I tried the door. The house was old and there was some play in it. I wrenched the door back and forth, jerking it in its frame.

"Charles, will you open the goddamned door, please!" I was frustrated, not only because I felt I was being ignored, but because of Charles's entire history of sleeping in – how many times had I found myself in this same situation, knocking on a door, ready to go out and face the world, while Charles dozed peacefully upstairs?

There was some give in the door, more in the pull than in the push. I wrenched it back and forth, working myself up into a froth. I would yank the door off its hinges, if necessary.

I imagined him upstairs, still in bed, dreaming away. He had probably, after I had dropped him off, spent hours online reading about old video games (for his generation, there was less of a division between high and low culture and things such as video games were the subject of serious thought). He had nowhere to be, nothing to do – no job, no wife, no children. His existence was a long, seamy gaze into a mirror, the mind a playground replete with his thoughts and memories unencumbered by responsibility. It was the ultimate retreat and it had gone wrong.

If I had to, I would stomp upstairs to his bedroom, pull him bodily out of his bed and march him to go get breakfast, just like normal people do at eight o'clock on a Saturday morning. And at breakfast I would give him a talking-to. I would hold back nothing in the hope that I could set him on a respectable path once and for all. No more late nights, no more empty hours to fritter away with thoughts of the lighthouse.

Suddenly, my efforts paid off and the door jerked open, spilling me onto my backside. There was a dry shifting, a hiss at the threshold of hearing, as the contents of the living room spilled through the door at my feet.

Sand. Beach sand, pure and unsullied, came through the living room door, stopping just as its grains started to cover my feet. I got up and stepped toward the living room. In the doorway, I surveyed the portion of the house that I could see – the living room that led to the dining room, the stairs on the left leading up.

The floor was covered with sand, so much so that if I were to set foot in the living room it would easily reach my calf. The sand receded into the depths of the house in gentle waves, much like the dunes that bordered the lake. In the living room, the couch, loveseat, end table, and an acoustic guitar were half-buried; beyond that, in the dining room, the table and chairs peeked out from a swell in the sand, like some remnant of a world reclaimed by nature. To the left, the wooden staircase, lacquered darkly, rose, the blonde sand spilled downward from the upstairs in a glacial waterfall; gravity, it seemed, had distributed the sand so that the bulk of it rested on the main floor.

"Charles," I called. "Are you all right?"

The sand deadened my voice. I stepped inside, sand squeaking under the soles of my shoes, and mounted the stairs. I held the banister for fear of falling, calling my brother's name as I climbed. There was no answer. On the second floor, the sand was shallower, nothing more than a thin layer. I opened the door to my brother's old bedroom. It was much as I remembered it with two shabby twin mattresses directly on the floor, a couple of old posters for musicians whose heyday had long since passed, an old Apple computer – but no sign of my brother. I checked the bathroom and master bedroom, into which he seemed to have relocated without bothering to clean up the time capsule of his old, cramped bedroom.

There was his father's king-size bed, sheets in a tangle. An old CRT television on the dresser with a VCR/DVD combo on top of it, the faint odor of stale tobacco smoke, and the sand. Again, my brother was nowhere to be found.

A thorough search of the house failed to locate him. The only thing left to do was leave. On the porch, however, his journal sat wedged in his stack of books. I extracted it from the pile and sat on the run-down couch. Outside, the sun was shining and the waxy leaves shimmered in the breeze. I noticed his pouch of tobacco and disposable lighter were still on the end table. If he was gone, he seemed to have left in haste. I opened the journal and began to read.

It was like any you'd expect, with thought fragments, confessional passages, ideas for songs and stories. I skimmed ahead, looking for any mention of the lighthouse in the hope that it would elucidate matters somehow. It wasn't long before I found it. There were a couple of preliminary sketches of the structure, done in my brother's competent crosshatch. If he had wanted to, he could have been a skilled artist. Instead, he opted for the life of a dilettante, dabbling here and there. I am not sure I'm giving him enough credit, for he showed remarkable ability in almost anything he delved into. Things, of course, that were difficult to exploit for any monetary gain. In his younger years, I used to encourage him in all of these areas, for they were also areas of personal interest. I had frittered away many hours with a guitar in my lap or my journal open in front of me, but the day came when I put it all away for good. I still look back fondly on those times – they had a time and a place – but I knew that I could never make anything of myself in the artistic realm. I again fell into the role of parent, wondering when my brother was going to put away all such silliness (or at least accept it for what it was) and settle down, find steady work, get married and all the rest.

So I wouldn't have to worry about him. Doesn't it always boil down to that? We truly hate to burden ourselves with unconventional people and any concern for their wellbeing is often just a subterfuge for the fact that we do not want to be inconvenienced by having to worry about them or, if we perhaps get lost and begin in an unguarded moment to daydream, try to puzzle out their motivations for why they choose to live the way they do. Is Charles only valuable in that he is productive? Is a person who does nothing somehow less than?

And in that instant I resented both our shared mother and his father for boiling him down to a potential cog in a machine, and myself for my complicity in trying to shape him into something he was not.

I read:

*When I think of the lighthouse, I sometimes have trouble seeing it as anything other than a symbol. Phallic associations aside, it belongs, at least in my mind, to the realm of a personal symbol (or local symbol?) rather than something larger or belonging to a collective unconscious [actually, this proves to be true – change].*

*In the local sense, it is a symbol of my childhood, a red sentry that has forever guarded the frontier of our community. It is also a symbol of direction, a beacon and if you ask my brother (or any other member of my family or even the community at large), you will find that I have built a reputation as having no sense of direction. Perhaps it appears that way – and for many years it was indeed the case, before I awakened to the lighthouse and all of its wonders.*

*I was constantly being compared to my brother, once as famous a layabout as myself, before he one day, out of the blue, decided to clean up his act and join respectable society. I remember when he told me he was moving away, taking a job that a friend in Portland had helped him secure (he had neither the education nor experience to secure such a position on his own, I believe). It was an "opportunity" he "couldn't pass up" (his words). He assured me that it was a temporary measure – that he was certain he was "bound to fail" – and that he would move back as soon as he could, that he would miss me and the thought of leaving pained him to no end. He was "wholly unqualified" to be doing the work he was doing and was sure to be exposed as a counterfeit before long.*

I remembered that conversation. My brother, able to pull quotes, apparently did too. I remembered the anxiety I felt at the time. I was young, inexperienced; the thought of leaving terrified me, and it pained me to have to be apart from Charles. But at the time, I felt I was at a crossroads. I had been unable to hold down a job – I too had been a master at shirking the responsibilities of adulthood. I was mired in a world of books, of what in my mind amounted to torrid love affairs (often with serious-minded women who had definite career goals toward which they were steadily working). It was a life of the mind, one in which I was free to daydream simply because I had the time – I needn't come up from these prolonged reveries for days at a time. My habits were irregular; I ate when I felt like it, slept when I felt like it. No one had me, body or mind, for long enough to interrupt this delicious delirium.

An image asserted itself in my mind, that of a person suspended in darkness, mouth shaped in a silent scream, arms outstretched as if grasping for a buoy in the nothingness. I did not recognize the features at first, though they bore an uncanny familiarity. A new soul had joined the ranks of those inexorably pulled away. I had thought it at first to be Charles, though cleanly shaven. I soon realized the receding figure was none other than myself, being pulled away from myself and everybody I had ever known.

I had neglected to shut the door. Sand, now unfettered by the barrier, had begun to slowly spill into the porch. There was already enough in the doorway to prevent the door from being closed again. I eyed my brother's pouch of tobacco and thought what the hell? I opened it and, twisting my body so that I could use the surface of the end table, rolled a cigarette. It was a bent affair and too plump in the middle. Any skill I had developed in my youth had since deteriorated. I lit up and inhaled. It was harsher than I expected but I did not cough. My head swam. My empty stomach grumbled. I continued smoking as I read:

*There had been speculation that Prendergast had lost his mind. It isn't mentioned in any of the mainstream history books (of which, given our town's puniness, there is a paucity) but if one goes to the library and sorts through the microfiche, one can find a Tribune article from 1870 that talks of a standoff at the lighthouse involving Prendergast. The police force, which back then consisted of two, tried in vain to remove him from the lighthouse, inside of which he claimed to have found the doorway to Paradise. One of the officers was injured by a volley of birdshot from one of Prendergast's hunting rifles. It was perhaps the officer's good luck that P did not have a penchant for bigger game.*

And, later:

*My brother has direction, one would say. I both envy it and resent it. But I know he suffers for it, that he would rather break free. I'm going to find a place for him, for both of us. I'm going to scout ahead and when I find it I'm going to take him with me. Is there something greater inside those intimate curving walls? I fear that this world can yield nothing new, that the only joy to be had lies in the endless repetition of phenomena that have already passed. To this I will surrender with an exhausted dull pleasure. To the lighthouse I go. To the lighthouse I have always gone and to the lighthouse I will always go.*

Despite my belief to the contrary, my foray into the respectable world was becoming a permanent groove into which the essence of my life was being poured. I had thrown away a decade and I was in danger of throwing away another and another and another. How greedily had I pursued all the baubles that were dangled in front of me. How readily, in trying to transmit the ideals in which I held no belief, had I forgotten the simple pleasures of idleness. I was suspended in air, mouth shaped into a silent scream, being pulled away from everyone and everything I had ever known. I longed to lie back and plunge into the delicious indolence that had bit by bit been removed from my life, as if by a flock of nervous birds pecking at a pile of seed. I thought of the lighthouse, my brother's lighthouse. Unlike the house he had inherited, it was not packed with the wonders and trinkets of childhood, but a cold and empty structure with oversized bolts and ample opportunity for the careless to bash their head on a seam of over-painted iron. I thought of the lighthouse, a submarine stood on end with walls sweating water and diluted rust, a roguish eye sweeping the roiling dark clouds above a choppy black lake. I thought of the lighthouse, now decorated with chairs, rugs, lamps and pictures on the wall and my brother peering through his eyeglasses at an open book with studious intent as the musical waves sloshed on the pier, I put down the journal and stubbed out the cigarette. I stepped outside into the bright day that was shaping up to disappoint the beachgoers with the crispness of its gathering winds.  I pointed myself in the direction of the lake and began walking toward the lighthouse, where I would live with my brother forever.

Jeremy Schliewe was born in Michigan and now lives in Tucson, Arizona. His short fiction has appeared in *Supernatural Tales*. His psychedelic pop band Harsh Mistress has two albums available from Burger Records. He produces music for film and video under the name Eidolon.